CARRY ME!

ROSEMARY WELLS

HYPERION BOOKS FOR CHILDREN

NEW YORK

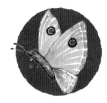

Printed in Hong Kong

First edition

1 2 3 4 5 6 7 8 9 10

Reinforced binding

Library of Congresss Cataloging-in-Publication Data on file.

ISBN 0-7868-0396-7

Visit www.hyperionbooksforchildren.com

For Zoë Helen and Eleanor Scarlett

Carry You,

Talk to You,

Sing to You . . .

CARRY ME!

Hold me up to the window
When Daddy comes down the street.

Carry me up the stairs and down.

Hold me while you get dressed for town.

Carry me into the garden
Under the plum tree's shadow.

Carry me over to hear the bees.
Stuff my pocket with early peas.

Carry me over the river.
Carry me under the sea.

Twirl me away in the evening air.

Fall asleep with me in your chair.

TALK TO ME!

Little blue light outside my door.

Sun makes circles on my floor.

Red eyes blink from busy wings.

Tell me a story about these things.

Green apple, sour.
Red apple, sweet.

How many shoes are on my feet?

How many feet are in my shoe?

What is the first thing I must do?

Open the window to hear the train.
Close the window against the rain.

Cold wind, east. Warm wind, west.
Who is the one that I love best?

Little blue light outside my door.
Silver circles on my floor.

Red eyes blink from moonlit wings.
Tell me a story about these things.

SING TO ME!

Sing me a winter song

I'll sing you right along

The old song we know

About the Wild Winter Wizard

With his beard full of blizzard
And his bags full of snow.

Sing me an April song
I'll hum you right along
Everywhere we go.

If you don't recall the words,
We'll ask the hummingbirds,
They're sure to know.

Sing me a summer song
I'll dance you right along
Bring out the spoons

Shake out the dancing rugs
We'll hop like lightning bugs
On the first of June.

Dancing so fancy-free,
Like stars in the grass we'll be
Under a harvest moon.